Losing My Virginity

Contents

Chapter 1 – Almost 18

Becca was in her room with her best friend Jenn. Becca was just one week away from turning 18.

"So are you excited for the party this weekend?" asked her best friend Jenn.

"Yea! Should be fun!" she replied.

"What's wrong? You don't seem too pumped about it! You can legally drink now!" she said.

"I know! It's just. God I don't know!" she said.

"Spill it! I've been your best friend since we were 5, what's wrong!" said Jenn.

Becca let out a deep sigh.

"I'm still a virgin!" she said.

"That's not that big of a deal. You've invited half the school, there will be lots of guys to choose from! That is easily fixed, if that's what you want!" she said trying to comfort her friend.

"Yea, I know. I have had offers, but honestly, I don't want my first time to be some high school kid who doesn't know what the fuck he's doing. Slide his dick in and two seconds later he gets his rocks off and I haven't even gotten wet yet!" she said placing her head into the palm of her hand.

"So, what are you saying, you want an older man to take your cherry?" she asked.

"Possibly! I've thought about it. But try to find a single, good looking, older man that is willing to fuck an 18 year old. If they are single, they aren't good looking. If they are good looking, they aren't single!" she replied.

"Do you care? I mean this is a onetime deal right? As long as he keeps his mouth shut, who cares!" she said.

"Sadly, I do. My parents raised me with morals. And knowing my luck, the guy's wife would find out and I would be a home wrecker! I can't live with that!" she said.

"I have an idea! It is super far outside the box. But, if you hear me out, I think you might love it!" she said.

"I'll listen! Shoot!" said Becca.

"Remember my cousin Paulo?" she asked.

"The creepy one?" replied Becca.

"Yea! That's him. He works in the adult film industry. What if, I got him to get you a male porn star to take your virginity! You would get a hot guy, who could fuck a long time, and it would be memorable!" she said.

"Are you fucking insane?" asked Becca.

"It's either that or take your pick of the boys at your party on Saturday!" she said.

Becca became silent and thought about her idea.

"Do you think he could arrange it?" asked Becca.

"I can contact him and find out! But if I ask, you have to be one hundred percent willing to go through with it! Fair?" said Jenn.

Becca thought for a few moments before replying.

"Deal! If he can get a good looking porn star, and I mean I want abs and muscles. Then I will let him take my virginity. But I want a pic of the dude before I agree to anything!" said Becca.

Jenn squealed in excitement.

"OK, I will call him tonight and let you know what he says!" said Jenn.

"You are fucking crazy! But I love you! This is actually a really good idea!" replied Becca.

"Can I watch him fuck you?" said Jenn.

"NO! Fuck! I will be nervous enough as it is!" said Becca.

"Aww!" said Jenn. "Listen, I have to run. I will let you know who you will be fucking later!" said Jenn.

"God, it sounds so bad when you put it that way!" she replied.

"You love it!" said Jenn.

"A little!" Said Becca with a smile. "I will see you later!" she added.

Jenn left and Becca got changed for bed. She turned out her bedroom light and hopped under the covers. She felt wrestles and unable to relax. She placed a hand between her legs and started to play with her clit. She found an orgasm before bed relaxed her just enough to let her fall asleep. Even though she was a virgin, she found clitoris stimulation was all she needed to orgasm. And she had been playing with herself for years.

She began rubbing her clit slowly. Her nipples instantly became rock hard as her body quickly became turned on and horny. She spread her legs wide as her fingers slowly rubbed her swollen clit. Her free hand grabbed her D-cup tits and pinched her nipples. She could feel her juices building between her legs and her clit becoming harder and more sensitive. She moaned to herself softly. Her mind started to wander as she thought about a hot porn star that would be deflowering her. She pictured a tall, dark and handsome man, covered in muscles and tattoos. In her mind he had a big fat cock that would surely hurt when he entered her. Her pussy juices started to trickle out of her body. She started to wonder how much his big cock would hurt as he pushed it deep into her body. She wondered if she would be able to suck him, and how much of that cock would fit into her mouth.

She grabbed her tit hard, wishing it was her porn star man handling her breast. She spread her legs wider and slid just the tip of her middle finger into her slippery hole. Her entire body shook as she started to cum hard.

She could feel her juices dripping from her body as her mind continued to think about this mystery man.

She lay in her bed panting. Her body aching and craving so much more. But for now, the edge was off. She would be able to sleep for now.

Chapter 2 – The Day Before The Party

Becca woke up the next day and headed downstairs.

She poured herself a cup of coffee and sat at the kitchen table alone. Her phone chimed with a new incoming text.

> *He has agreed! Here are two porn stars to choose from.*

She looked at the two attachments. Both men were quite attractive and fully naked. Both were quite well endowed. But the one man with the short brown hair and tattoos up both arms and rock hard abs and a very developed body sent shivers through her body and instantly made her pussy wet.

She quickly sent a reply.

> *I'll take contestant number two. He is fucking dreamy!!!*

She looked at his picture again and started to fantasize about his cock inside her. She was quickly overcoming her nerves and started to get very excited about this upcoming event.

Her phone chimed again.

> *I knew you would choose him. Paulo says Saturday at 1 PM. You need to sign a waiver saying you give permission for this guy to fuck you. After that, you are getting laid!*

She smiled as her heart skipped a beat. She was going to lose her virginity on her actual birthday.

> *I can sign a waiver. No issues!*

She had a sip of her coffee as she looked at his picture again.

> *Excellent. I will finalize the arrangements with Paulo. You are one lucky bitch!*

She smiled as she read the latest text and replied.

> *Jealous? LOL*

There was a pause before the next text came in.

Little bit! I still want to watch!

Becca rolled her eyes.

I don't know Jenn! I can't believe I am doing this, never mind putting on a show!

She finished her coffee and put the cup in the sink. She went back upstairs to get dressed when her phone chimed again.

At least you didn't say no this time. I am begging! PLEASE let me watch! I'm your best friend!!! Pretty please?

Becca threw her phone on the bed. She tossed her nighty in the laundry hamper and slid on her black thong and matching bra.

Her phone chimed again.

Please! I will do anything!!

Becca thought for a moment before replying. She was trying to process everything that was happening. It was a little overwhelming. But she thought to herself, this would be a once in a lifetime opportunity. Not only would she be fucking an insanely hot porn star, but her best friend wants to watch.

She quickly typed in a reply.

Define anything!

She tossed her phone on the bed again as she pulled up her jeans and put on her favorite V-neck sweater that showed off her tits perfectly.

Her phone chimed again.

Literally anything. Name your price – I want to see you get fucked by a porn star.

Becca's mind started to think about what she could do to make this worthwhile. She figured the fuck would last an hour, maybe two tops. Then they would have a few hours to kill before the party later that night.

There were no secrets between the two of them. She knew Jenn had broken up with her boyfriend a while ago and she was currently looking for someone new. She wanted to use this to her advantage somehow. A naughty idea entered her head as she sent a reply.

Saturday night. I pick the guy, you can join me in fucking him. We do a threesome, but it's my choice who it is, and it's my rules!

She tossed her phone down and looked at herself in the mirror. She adjusted her tits so they were perfectly center and on display. She applied her make-up, lipstick and perfume. Her phone went off one more time

FUCKING SLUT!!! I accept your offer! LOL

A huge smile came across her face as she typed in a reply.

You're the slut! You just agreed to fuck me!

Becca had been bi-curious ever since she started masturbating and had wanted to kiss her friend Jenn for a long time. But she was too scared to bring it up, so this was the perfect time to get what she wanted.

I've been wanting to fuck you for a long time! I can't wait for Saturday! XOXO

Becca could not believe her reply. Her best friend wanted to fuck her as much as she wanted to fuck Jenn.

Saturday is going to be EPIC! Thank you for the great idea! I can't wait XOXO

Becca left the house and went to do her errands she had lined up for the day. She had a few things her mom had asked her to pick up for the party the next day.

Jenn returned home later that evening with the list of items her mom had asked for. She walked into the kitchen with the bags to find her mom and dad at the table having a conversation.

"Oh hey Becca! We were just talking about the party tomorrow! How was your day?" asked her mom.

"Great! Got what you asked for! So I think we are good to go!" she replied.

"Awesome! Thank you so much! I'm sorry to burden you with that but work has been so chaotic I just didn't have time!" said her mom.

"It's all good! So what were you discussing?" she asked.

"Oh, just that we will be there at the start of your party! But once everyone arrives your father and I will excuse ourselves. We are going to rent a room and let you have fun! Don't destroy the place is all we ask!" she said.

"Cool! It will be pretty low key. I know everyone who is coming quite well. So you won't have to worry!" said Becca.

"What are you doing tomorrow prior to the party?" asked her father out of the blue.

Becca froze for a second. She could not tell them she was meeting a porn star to fuck her and deflower her. She had to think fast.

"Jenn is coming over around noon to take me to lunch. Happy birthday to me! I think she is trying to surprise me with something. So I am just playing along!" said Becca.

"Oh how lovely! Jenn is so thoughtful. She is such a wonderful young lady!" said her mother.

"Anyway, I am going to head upstairs and watch some Netflix and crash! I want to be well rested for tomorrow!" said Becca.

"Good night sweetie. Love you!" said her father.

"Love you both! See you in the morning!" said Becca as she walked up the stairs.

She closed the door to her room and put on a loose fitting tank top. She crawled into bed and thought about the next day. She was excited beyond measure, but also very nervous. She grabbed her phone and looked at the picture Jenn sent. Butterflies filled her body as she thought about that hunk of a man taking her virginity the very next day. She looked at his cock slid her free hand between her legs. She slid her middle finger into her pussy and could feel she was soaked. She began to play with her pussy, teasing it slowly. She pushed her middle finger into herself as far as she could as she focused on that cock. She knew his cock would be much larger than her finger and she wondered how much it was going to hurt. She teased her clit with her soaking wet finger. Her eyes half closing as her body quickly neared its climax. Her fingers rubbing her clit hard and fast as her breathing became heavy. Her legs spread wide as in her mind she could almost feel the hunk of that man entering her. She could almost feel his kisses and his breath on her neck.

Her pussy erupted. She came harder than she had ever cum before. She lay in the center of her bed gasping for air. Her entire body shaking from her hard orgasm.

She took one more look at her phone and kissed the screen good night.

Chapter 3 – Nervous

Becca spent extra time getting ready for her appointment. She had a long shower and made sure her entire body was shaved perfectly smooth. She double and triple checked her pussy to make sure not one hair was missed. She spent almost an hour in front of her mirror applying her make-up and lipstick. She dabbed on her favorite perfume and put on her favorite black lace bra and matching thong. She picked out her black mini skirt and a dark blue button up top to which she purposefully left the top three buttons undone so the trim of her black bra could be seen.

She took a minute to admire herself in her full length mirror before going downstairs. She looked amazing. She knew heads would turn her way today and she loved it.

She knew today was a setup, and there would be no emotion to what was going to happen. But she could not help wanting him to be attracted to her and really want to fuck her and not be just another piece of ass to him.

Jenn arrived at Becca's just after noon.

"Hey hon! Wow! You look fucking sexy!" said Jenn.

"Thank you! I am not sure why I put so much effort in, clothes won't stay on long!" she said.

Jenn laughed.

"You are probably right, but still. You look fucking hot!" replied Jenn. "Are you ready for this?" she added.

"Absolutely! Let's go!" Replied Becca.

They hopped into the car and Jenn was about to drive off before Becca touched her arm and looked at her.

"Listen, before we go, can I ask you one question?" said Becca with her nerves in overdrive.

"Anything! You know that!" replied Jenn.

"Have you really wanted to fuck me for a long time?" asked Becca.

Jenn smiled. She leaned over and looked Becca in the eyes. And without saying a word gave her a long lustful French kiss. Their tongues met and played in each other's mouths for a few minutes as they enjoyed their very first kiss together.

"Yes! I can't wait to fuck you tonight. And to be honest, I don't care if there is a guy joining us or not. It's your birthday, it's your call. But if ends up being just you and me, that's cool too. Fair?" she replied.

"I love you! Can I have one more kiss before we do this?" Asked Becca.

Jenn leaned in for another kiss. This time as they kissed Becca slid her hand on to Jenn's breast and gave it a firm squeeze.

"Let's go get you fucked!" said Jenn.

She put the car into gear and drove off.

Chapter 4 – Cherry Popping

Jenn and Becca arrived at the studio just before 1 PM. They walked in and Paulo was there to greet them.

"Jenn baby! Always great to see you!" he said as he looked at her tits.

He gave her a kiss on each cheek.

"You must be Becca." He said as he shook her hand and looked at her tits.

"So has Jenn explained how this works?" he asked.

"I think so. Not really. Sorry, I am a little nervous." She said.

All of a sudden she was so nervous her entire body was shaking. A small voice in her head was telling her to run. But the rest of her body was so ready and excited for this that it was easy to turn off that voice.

"Simple. You sign a waiver saying that you agree for Blake to fuck you. And you guarantee that you are a virgin. We capture it all on film and you receive five percent of the royalties. Which in this business is good money for your first action shot. But I am offering that to you because it's a virginity shoot. This will sell like fucking hotcakes." He said.

"Wait! Film? I didn't know we'd be filming this!" She said.

"Babe listen. The cameras roll on your tits and ass and close ups on his cock fucking you. Few minutes into the action and you won't even see the camera's I promise you. Plus if this goes as well as I think it will, you stand to make an easy 10 grand or more!" he said trying to calm her nerves.

"Now, if you will sign here, I can introduce you to Blake and we can go over the story line!" he said.

"Story line?" she questioned.

"Every porno has a story line. Well a short one anyway. Time is money ladies. Are we doing this?" asked Paulo.

Becca grabbed the form and filled out her name, address and signed the bottom.

"Jenn, do you want to witness this?" he said as he handed the form to Jenn.

Jenn signed on the line beside Becca's signature.

"Excellent. Now if you ladies will follow me!" said Paulo.

They walked through the door to the right of reception and followed him down a hallway to another door. Behind that door was a large filming area where there were a variety of shooting areas. One was a simple bedroom, one was setup like a dungeon with restraints on the walls and a number of whips and flogs hanging on the wall. Another area was setup as an outdoor park. There were cameras and people everywhere. Becca grabbed Jenn's hand and held it tight. Jenn could feel her palm sweating as they held hands.

"Relax, it's going to be ok!" whispered Jenn.

"Blake! Where the fuck are you?" shouted Paulo.

From around one of the corners came a face she recognized. It was the man in the photo on her phone. Although he was clothed, she did look at his face enough times that she recognized him.

"Blake, this is Becca and my cousin Jenn. Becca will filming with you today." He said.

Blake took an obvious look up and down her body and smiled.

"It's nice to meet you Becca!" he said as he took the back of her hand and kissed it softly. "I am looking forward to taking your cherry!" he said as he looked into her eyes.

Becca could hardly form a sentence. She was nervous and at a loss for words staring into this gorgeous man's eyes.

"I, uh, hi! Nice to meet you. Yes, you will, I mean, I'm looking forward to it. Sorry, I'm nervous!" she said clumsily.

Blake smiled as he admired her body again taking an extended noticeable look at her tits.

"OK! So here is the concept. The shoot will start on the bed. Becca you will have your shirt open more so we can clearly see your bra. Blake you will be topless. We will start with a little chatter about how special this will be, yadda yadda yadda, you'll start kissing and we will go from there!" Said Paulo. "Any Questions?" he added.

Becca looked over to Blake who had already removed his shirt. She bit her bottom lip as she admired his rock hard muscular body.

"May I?" asked Blake.

"Sorry?" questioned Becca.

"We need to unbutton more of your shirt!" he replied.

"Oh! Yes. Do what you need to me!" she said trying to be flirtatious.

Blake smiled at her again and unbuttoned all but one button on her shirt.

"Let's go to the bed!" he said.

He grabbed her hand and interlocked his fingers with hers. Becca walked beside him letting him take full control.

He sat on the edge of the bed and tapped the bed where he wanted Becca to sit.

"Try and relax. I will take the lead in the conversation. Just answer with whatever comes to your mind. Don't over think it, just roll with it. The conversation will be short. Then I'll kiss you and start to play with your tits. Don't undo my pants until after I have you naked. You will hear Paulo shout commands, follow the commands. Don't worry, the sound engineers make sure his whiny voice is never in the final product." Said Blake giving her instructions.

Becca nodded her head and took a deep breath.

"Are you ready?" asked Blake.

"Ready as I will ever be!" she said.

Blake nodded to Paulo.

"ACTION!" shouted Paulo.

"Hey baby! I can't believe it's our three month anniversary! Our time together has been beyond perfect." He said as he rubbed her shoulder.

"I know! I've really enjoyed our time! Let's take it to the next step!" she replied.

"CUT! NO NO NO!" shouted Paulo. "This whole anniversary thing is so cliché. Blake, make it more modern! High school sweethearts, parents away for the weekend, something like that!" said Paulo.

"Got it boss!" replied Blake as he looked at Becca and smiled. "Relax. Take a deep breath!" he said noticing her nervousness.

Becca melted into his eyes again. Every time she looked at his steely blue eyes everything around her disappeared and all she could see was him.

"ACTION!" shouted Paulo.

"Hey babe! I'm so happy your parents are gone for the weekend. Now we can have some fun without worrying about being caught!" he said.

"I know! I'm so excited!" she said as she looked into his eyes.

"Are you sure you're ready?" he asked her.

Becca knew that was the virginity question. Her body was on fire for this man. She wanted nothing more in the world than his cock inside of her, no matter how much it might hurt.

"God yes baby! I've dreamed of this night for a long time now!" she replied.

Blake said nothing more but kissed her. The room spun around her as she felt his tongue slid into her mouth. She placed her hand on his pectoral muscle as she felt his hand unbutton the last button on her shirt. His hand came to rest on her breast as he gave it a firm squeeze.

The butterflies inside of Becca were going insane. Her heart was beating through her chest as her tongue played with Blake's. Blake slowly removed Becca's top and tossed it to the floor. He continued to kiss her as he slid his hand up her skirt to expose her black panties. Becca didn't even notice the camera man just a few feet away from them zooming in on Blake's fingers pushing her panties aside as he teased her clit.

She was lost in the moment as Blake snapped his fingers on her bra and released the clasps holding her breasts hostage. He slowly removed it from her body and tossed it to the floor. His hand came up from her legs and began fondling her breasts. They continued to kiss lustfully as his fingers pinched her nipples making the hard. Blake for the first time broke the kiss so he could take her breast in his mouth. He began sucking on it as the tip of his tongue teased her nipple. Becca tilted her head back and moaned softly as she let Blake do as he pleased to her body. He sucked her other nipple and teased it with his tongue. Blake began kissing his way down her body until he reached her skirt. He unzipped the back of her skirt and removed it from her body as she lay on the bed in just her black thong. Blake crawled up beside her and kissed her again. His hand inside of her panties as she felt his middle finger enter her body. Her pussy was dripping wet as his finger easily slid in and out of her body. Becca wrapped her arms around his neck getting lost in the moment. She loved the way he kissed her. Her pussy was enjoying his finger inside her body. Nothing else mattered right now but how he was making her feel.

Blake pushed her panties off her body and tossed them aside. She lay in the bed completely naked as he continued to kiss her.

"Ok Becca, start removing Blake's pants!" she head Paulo direct.

Becca almost forgetting where she was as she got a little snap of reality.

Her hand reached for his jeans as she unbuttoned them and unzipped them. She slid her hand into his jeans and felt his big fat cock ready to go. Her heart raced as she wanted to badly to jump on top of him. But she knew that Blake would lead her through this uncharted territory of hers.

Slowly she removed his jeans and his boxers. He lay in bed naked with her. She placed her hand on his rock hard cock and stroked it slowly, unsure what else to do.

"Becca baby, suck his dick now!" came the order from Paulo.

Becca broke the kiss and moved so she was hovering over his dick. It looked so much bigger in person than the picture on her phone. Her hand slowly stroked the base as she took the head into her mouth. Blake brushed her long brunette hair to the side so the camera could get a good shot of her head bouncing up and down on his cock. Her hand choked the base of his cock and stroked it in rhythm of her mouth sliding up and down his dick. Each time she took as much of his cock as she could into her mouth. She felt his head pushing at the back of her throat. She realized she could only comfortably handle half of his cock in her mouth and she could not help but wonder how he would feel inside of her. Blake could feel her saliva running down the base of his shaft. Becca used her saliva as lubrication with her hand as she continued stroking the base of his dick. She head Blake let out a moan as she continued to suck off his big fat dick. The butterflies returned as the felt she was pleasing him with her inexperienced talent. His fingers grabbed a handful of her hair as he pulled it aside, making sure the camera had a good angle to capture her sucking his cock.

"Blake baby! Time to take her cherry!" announced Paulo.

Becca stopped sucking him and returned to lay beside Blake. He kissed her softly and whispered into her ear so only she could hear "Relax baby!"

Becca was nervous, but tried to relax.

Blake positioned himself between her legs and ran the head of his cock over her very swollen clit. She looked up at him and into his blue eyes. His eyes seemed to calm her and make her feel relaxed. She felt Blake run the tip of his head over her opening. He slapped his cock against her clit a few time sending shivers through her body. She wanted him to enter her. She didn't care how much it might hurt. She needed him inside of her desperately.

Blake pushed the head into her body. Becca gasped a little as she had never been stretched like that before.

Blake pulled out and rubbed the head over her clit again. He looked down at her young body, her rock hard nipples and the lust in her eyes. He watched as she bit her bottom lip looking up at him. He could see the need in her eyes. He pushed his cock back into her, a little further this time. The head of his cock meeting the wall as he left his cock there for a moment for her to get used to it.

A look of discomfort came over her face as he slowly slid his dick in and out of her entrance. Each time stopping as he hit the wall.

He leaned over and placed his hand on her head and whispered softly into her ear.

"Here we go, spread your legs and relax baby girl!" he whispered.

Becca spread her legs as wide as they would go. The name baby girl made her feel special. A camera man stood behind Blake and bent down so he had the perfect angle of his cock sliding into her the entire way for the very first time.

Blake pushed against her wall and pushed through it. Becca let out a little squeal as her wall was penetrated for the first time. She wrapped her arms around her neck and kissed him hard to distract herself from the discomfort. Blake pushed his cock all the way into her body as they kissed lustfully.

He let his cock stay deeply inserted into her as they kissed. Allowing her body to get used to his size and girth.

"How does that feel baby?" he asked.

"I'm good! Don't stop baby!" she said as her breathing was a little heavy.

Blake started to slide his cock in and out of her slippery wet chasm. She was very tight, but her ample juices gave him the lubrication he needed to start fucking her slowly. Becca found herself biting her bottom lip again as she looked up at her lover. His cold steely blue eyes taking all the pain away as his cock picked up speed. Blake looked down and saw her full breasts bouncing wildly as he started to fuck her hard and deep. He could feel her juices covering his cock as he now easily slid in and out of her body. He leaned over and kissed her deep as his cock continued to fill her fiery chasm.

The discomfort was gone, the pain was long forgotten as all that Becca's body could feel was ecstasy. She could not believe how amazing this felt to have this stud fucking her hard.

Becca started screaming loudly. The camera man got another close up of Blake's dick pounding Becca hard as she clearly was having her first orgasm from a cock.

"YES! FUCK YES!" She screamed out loudly.

Her pussy was soaked. The entire area between her legs was glistening in her juices. Blake continued to pound her hard through her orgasm. Her pussy easy to fuck now as it was coated in her climactic release.

Once he saw her body relaxing as her climax subsided, he asked her to roll over and get on her hands and knees.

Becca followed his instruction. He helped put her in the right position by pressing his hand on her upper back signaling her to put her face into the pillow. Her ass was pointed to the air and her knees were wide apart as she felt him enter her again. Her body was not completely recovered from her first orgasm as she felt his strong manly hands grab her hips and start fucking her hard and fast. The room was filled with an audible slap as their bodies slammed together with every hard fucking thrust into her dripping wet hole. All Becca could do was scream into the pillow in delight. She could feel her juices dripping down the inside of her leg as the well experienced porn star went to work on her creamy hole. His cock slamming deep into her body making her feel every inch of his nine inch cock stretching her hole wide. His right hand lifted to the air and came smashing down on her ass leaving a bright red hand print on her ass as his cock continued its assault on her pussy.

Becca grabbed the pillow under her head hard. Her pussy was a huge mess from her none stop juices flowing as Blake fucked her. She was becoming light headed from what he was doing to her body. She rested her head on the pillow and let him have his way with her pussy.

Blake nodded over to Paulo.

"Becca baby, time to suck some more cock!" was the command she heard.

She turned over quickly and opened her mouth. Blake placed his cock on her tongue and she felt his cum shoot into her mouth. She was taken back a little as she was not expecting him to cum yet. But she swallowed it and allowed his cum to shoot all over her tongue and chin. She looked into the camera and smiled as she felt his load splash against her cheek and slowly drip down the side of her face.

"And CUT!" Yelled Paulo. "Becca baby, you were fantastic!" he said.

Reality came rushing back to Becca as she looked around. There were four different guys with cameras on her shoulder and her friend Jenn standing off to the side with a monstrous grin on her face.

"What happens now?" asked Becca.

"We are done! The rest will be done by the editors and production crew. Final scene will be ready for review in a couple of weeks!" said Blake.

"Oh Ok!" replied Becca.

The one thing she had not thought about or prepared for was the sudden ending. They were done and Blake was already getting dressed. She felt a little empty inside, but at the same time she felt amazing as he had performed well beyond her expectations. And if nothing else she had a fantastic story to tell on how she lost her virginity.

Just then Blake walked up to her.

"You know. You were pretty good for a beginner. You should consider doing this full time. The money is fantastic, and you get as much sex as you can handle!" he said.

Becca was not expecting a job offer.

"Um, thank you? Do you think I did ok? I mean, honestly. You took my virginity. Not like I have a lot of experience here!" she replied.

"Put it this way, I would love to do a full length film with you. If you are interested, talk to Paulo and tell him you want another shoot. I'm game if you are!" he said.

He gave her a kiss on the lips and spanked her ass then walked away.

Just then Jenn came to her side.

"Fuck was that hot! How do you feel?" she asked.

"Little sore, but pretty fucking awesome! I don't even know how many times I came. I think it was one giant orgasm!" she said.

Becca picked up her clothes from the side of the bed and started to get dressed.

"Becca, you are a star in the making! You are a natural. We could use someone like you on the big screen. If you ever want to talk about more films!" said Paulo as he eyed her naked young body.

Becca put on her thong and her bra and smiled at Paulo.

"I am not sure about that. I appreciate the offer, but I kind of wanted to take a different career path!" she said faking a smile.

"Well the door is open if you change your mind! You'll receive your first check in about two months, then you will receive additional checks based on sales every month after that." He said. "Ok, that's a wrap. Let's clean up and get ready for the next shoot!" he said as he walked away from Becca.

Becca finished getting dressed and walked back to Jenn's car. They got in and Jenn looked over at her friend with a never ending grin.

"What?" she asked.

"You know what!" replied Jenn. "I want details!" she said.

"You were there, you watch the whole fucking thing! How can I give you any more details!" said Becca.

"How did his cock feel? He was fucking huge!" she said.

"It hurt at first. But he was gentle. Once we got through the original pain it wasn't so bad. And once I came, it started to feel fucking amazing!" she said.

"I'm almost jealous! God tonight is going to be so much fun!" said Jenn.

"You still want to fuck me?" taunted Becca with a smile on her face.

"More than anything in the world bitch!" she said as she leaned over and kissed her hard. Jenn's hand slid into Becca's bra and gave her breast a hard squeeze as they made out in the parking lot for a while.

Chapter 5 – 18th Birthday Party

Becca went upstairs and had a shower. She wanted to wash the scent of sex off of her body and change in her evening dress that she had purchased special for the party.

She came downstairs just before 7 PM as her parents were standing waiting for her at the bottom of the stairs.

"Wow! You are all grown up!" said her father standing there admiring his beautiful daughter as she slowly walked down the stairs.

"Thanks Daddy!" She said shyly.

"The punch and chips are out. The dips are ready for heating when you want them. Just pop them in the oven at 350 for 20 minutes!" said her mom.

"Thank you! You guys have been awesome! Thanks for letting me have this party!" she said.

Just then the door opened and Jenn walked in.

"Long time no see!" said Jenn as she looked at Becca.

"Where did you guys go for lunch?" Asked her father.

They both looked at each other with a blank look on their face.

"We went uptown to that Pizza place we love so much!" blurted Jenn.

"All the way uptown? That's a bit of a drive just for a pizza!" said her father.

"Well it is her birthday! Nothing is too good for my bestie!" said Jenn almost awkwardly.

"OK! We are off. You kids have fun! Behave! Don't burn the place down! But mostly have fun!" said her father.

"Thanks!" replied Becca.

She gave both her parents a hug as they left the house.

Becca and Jenn watched from the front window as they drove away.

"PARTY ON! So who's it going to be, have you decided yet?" asked Jenn.

"Who's it going to be for what?" asked Becca.

"To fuck us later!" she said.

"I'm not sure. Maybe Mike. I know he looks at my tits all the time and I am pretty sure he'd be down to fuck. He's kind of hot! Or possibly Dave. He's super nice and sweet and good looking. I think he would do literally anything we asked! We could dominate him together!" she said as she burst out into laughter.

"Pick Dave! I heard Mike has like no dick!" replied Jenn. "Plus you are right, we could dominate him! It would be total fun!" she added.

"Alright. I will make sure Dave stays until the end. Should I tell him he is fucking both of us, or just leave that as a surprise?" asked Becca.

"You're the birthday girl. You are in complete control. But, before anyone else arrives, kiss me!" said Jenn.

Becca did not have to be asked twice as she pulled Jenn into her arms and gave her a long lustful French kiss.

The doorbell rang and interrupted their kiss.

Becca walked to the door and let in a few of her girlfriends from school. She spent the next 45 minutes welcoming her friends into her parent's house.

The doorbell rang on last time and it was Dave at the door.

"Holy crap! You look stunning!" he said as he looked at Becca.

"Aww, Thank you Dave! You dress up pretty nice yourself!" she said.

Dave blushed. He had a small self-confidence issue and did not handle compliments well.

"Thanks!" he replied as his face turned red.

"Won't you please come in!" asked Becca.

"Thank you! Here, these are for you!" as he presented her with a bouquet of flowers from behind his back.

"Sorry, I did not know what to get, so I thought flowers were safe. I hope you don't mind!" he said softly.

"Aww, Dave! They are beautiful! So thoughtful. Thank you." She said as she smelled their scent. "I love them!" she added as she gave him a hug and a kiss on the cheek.

"Make yourself comfortable, I am just going to put these in a vase real quick!" she said.

Dave made his way to the living room and said hello to the people he knew. Jenn came up to him and said hello.

"Hey Dave! So glad you could come! How are you?" she asked.

"I'm good! Quite the turn out tonight!" he said as he looked over the crowded house.

"Yea, I don't suspect most of the people to stay too late." She said.

"Oh? Why is that?" he said nervously.

Dave always felt nervous talking to pretty women. Both Becca and Jenn were among the hottest girls in the school. Both had fantastic tits, both always wore low cut cleavage revealing tops and both had men drooling at their feet. He was not exactly sure why Jenn was talking to him now, as normally she would be with the jocks.

"I don't know. Just a feeling I get." She said. "Are you going to stay until the end?" she added.

"I hadn't thought about how long I would be staying. I could. Not like I have any other plans!" he said with a nervous laugh.

"Hang out! I will be fun!" She said.

"Um, Ok! Sure!" said Dave.

"I need another drink! I will be right back!" she said.

She walked by Dave who was standing in a doorway during their conversation. As she pushed by him she made sure that her breasts rubbed against his body.

Dave blushed as her breasts brushed against him.

He nervously took a sip of his drink and walked into the main living area.

Jenn walked into the kitchen and walked up to Becca who had just placed the flowers on the table.

"Who brought you flowers?" Asked Jenn.

"Dave! He is so sweet!" she said smiling.

"He is! And I just invited him to stay until the end of the party!" she said.

"Oh really? And what if I change my mind?" she said.

"You won't! I know you. But if you do we may have to invite two guys to hang out!" she said laughing.

"No! It's definitely going to be Dave. The flowers were very kind and thoughtful. He Is golng to get laid tonlght! No question!" said Becca.

"Good! So shall I hit on him all night then?" asked Jenn.

"I think we both should! Let's make sure he is hard and ready for us to use later!" she said with a laugh.

Becca walked back into the main area and found Dave. He was propped up against the wall looking around but not engaged in a conversation.

"Dave! There you are. I just wanted to thank you again for the flowers. They are so beautiful!" she said as she gave him a kiss on the cheek.

"Oh, you are welcome! Like I said I wasn't sure what was appropriate!" he said as he nervously as he had another drink.

"Well you are the only person here tonight that was thoughtful enough to bring me anything. So I will have to find a way to thank you!" she said as she winked at him.

Dave blushed again. He was a good looking guy, but spent most of his time on his studies and computers. He quickly became known as the geek of the school, and although he was highly intelligent, he never did figure out a way to be comfortable with the ladies.

"What are you drinking Dave?" she asked in a flirtatious voice?

"Vodka and Cranberry!" he replied.

"Let me get you a refill!" she said as she took his cup.

Becca poured a double vodka with a splash of cranberry mix. She figured a little liquid courage may go a long way in her after party plans with Dave.

"Here you go hon!" She said as she handed him his drink. "I hear Jenn asked you to stay till then end!" she added.

"Yes! She did!" he said as he took a sip of his drink. "Wow! That's good!" he said.

"I see a couple people leaving. I will be right back!" she said.

Becca went to the door and said goodbye to a few people who were leaving. Jenn took her cue and walked up to Dave to carry on the conversation.

"Dave, would you join me in the kitchen! Fix me a drink! I would love to try what you are drinking!" she said.

"Oh! Ok, Sure!" he said as he walked to the kitchen with Jenn.

"Do you like shooters Dave?" she asked.

"Some of them! Yes!" he replied.

"Good! Have you ever had a porn star?" she asked.

"No, actually. What's in it?" he asked.

"Raspberry sourpuss and Blue Curacao!" she said.

Jenn poured a bunch of both liquors into a shaker and poured out two shots. Becca walked into the kitchen just as she was pouring the second shot.

"What are you guys doing?" she asked.

"Becca! You are just in time. I am introducing Dave to Porn Stars!" replied Jenn.

Jenn poured a third shot and handed them all out. They all slammed the shot back.

"Wow! That is like Kool-Aid!" said Dave.

"Want to be a porn star Dave? I mean have another porn star?" Asked Jenn.

"I would love another one!" he said.

He was becoming less nervous with the ladies flirtatious advances as the alcohol brought down his walls.

Becca slammed one more back before returning to the front door to say good bye to some other friends.

As Dave put the shot glass on the kitchen table he happen to glance at Jenn's breasts. More by accident than on purpose, but she caught him staring.

"Do you like what you see, Dave?" she asked playfully.

Even the alcohol running through his system was not enough to stop him from blushing.

"I'm sorry, I meant no disrespect!" he said as he turned completely red.

"No disrespect sweetie! Be honest, do you like what you see?" she asked again.

He watched as Jenn smiled at him, waiting patiently for his answer.

"I will be honest. You are an incredibly beautiful woman. And yes, I very much like what I see!" he said softly.

"Good!" she said softly as she took a step closer to him.

"Do you want to touch them?" she whispered into his ear as she let them graze against his chest ever so slightly.

Dave's cock jumped to attention. He couldn't hide it and his face turned beet red. Jenn took his hand and placed it on her breast.

"Tell me what you are thinking!" she said.

Dave smiled at her, leaving his hand on her breast.

Becca walked back into the room and Dave quickly removed his hand like he was busted for doing something wrong.

"I see you two are getting along fine!" she said.

"Jenn can you make another round of porn stars?" she asked.

"For sure!" she replied.

Jenn started to make the drink as Becca walked up to Dave.

"So, tell me Dave, who has the nicer tits. Jenn? Or Me?" She asked as she placed his hand on her breast.

Dave was starting to figure out what the payment for the flowers was going to be. The alcohol was doing its job and he was starting to feel a little bold.

"Well, I am not sure! I may need to feel them at the same time!" he said with a mischievous grin appearing on his face.

Jenn didn't say a word but turned to him and came close enough that he could place his other hand on her breast.

"Oh, I do not know. This is a very hard choice. Both sets are magnificent. Do you mind if I take my time in my analysis. As a person with a very technical background I do not want to judge too quickly without collecting sufficient data!" he said.

Becca reached to his crotch and grabbed his cock through his pants.

"You are right Dave. This is very hard!" she said as she held on to it firmly.

Dave's hands were now running over both sets of breasts as he freely felt up the ladies trying to see who he would deem the winner.

"Let me see if I can persuade your decision a little!" said Becca.

She leaned into him and gave him a long lustful French kiss. Dave removed his hand from Jenn's tits and held Becca in his arms while they made out for a minute.

"I will be right back, there is only one couple left and I am going to see them out!" she said.

Becca walked to the front door and had a chat with the last remaining people at the party.

"I think it's hardly fair that she gets to cheat like that. I think I should have the same advantage!" said Jenn as she leaned in and kissed Dave lustfully.

As she kissed Dave she unzipped his jeans and pulled his throbbing cock out. She was happily surprised to see that he was very well endowed. She started to stroke it slowly as they made out in the kitchen.

Becca returned to see the action happening in the kitchen.

"You bitch! You are so cheating!" she said with a chuckle. "Everyone is gone, let's go upstairs!" she added.

Dave put his cock away and followed the ladies up to Becca's bedroom.

"Dave, it's my birthday, and I call the shots! Are you ok with that?" asked Becca.

Dave nodded his head, still in disbelief as to what was unfolding at this second.

"Good! Now, get undressed!" she ordered.

Dave unbuttoned his shirt and let it fall to the floor. He unfastened his jeans and removed them, then slid his boxer-briefs down as he stood before the two ladies completely naked.

Becca's eyes opened wide as she admired Dave's cock. It was not quite as big as Blake's but it was not far off.

"Jenn, you too! Undress bitch!" she said playfully.

"Yes Ma'am!" replied Jenn.

Jenn pulled her cleavage revealing top off and tossed it to the floor. Dave's eyes were glued to Jenn as she reached behind her back to unfasten the clasp to her floral pink bra. He watched it fall to the ground as her breasts were on display for him. Her nipples already rock hard as she pushed her leggings off her body only to reveal she was not wearing any panties.

"Aren't you the little slut with no panties!" laughed Becca.

"Dave be a dear and help me unzip my dress would you?" Becca asked as she turned her back to Dave.

Dave slowly unzipped her dress and Becca removed it. She placed it over a chair and proceeded to remove her bra and thong.

"Now, Dave lay on the bed!" commanded Becca.

"Jenn, you can slide that tight little pussy of yours on to that cock!" dictated Becca.

Dave got into place and Jenn wasted no time climbing on top of Dave. She positioned her pussy on top of his wet head and slowly impaled herself on to his fat cock. Jenn moaned a little as his cock filled her and stretched her.

Becca placed her pussy over Dave's face and lowered herself on to him until she could feel his lips were at her entrance. Dave wrapped his arms around the top of her legs as she felt his tongue lapping at her clit. She leaned forward and grabbed Jenn in her arms as she started to make out with Jenn. Jenn started to slide up and down Dave's dick slowly as they kissed.

Becca's pussy quickly became wet and Dave could taste her juices dripping on to his tongue as he attacked her clit. His tongue slid as deep as he could reach into her slippery hole as he savored her sweet nectar. Becca was impressed with his skills as his tongue quickly brought her body to a state of ecstasy. Becca's tongue explored the inside of Jenn's mouth as Jenn slid faster up and down on Dave's throbbing dick. Her hand reached up and started to fondle her friend's breasts as she pinched and tugged the nipples. Jenn was riding Dave hard now. She had to break the kiss to moan loudly as Dave was filling her crevice completely. Jenn held her hands on Becca's shoulders as she rode him hard and fast. Dave's tongue continued to lap at Becca's pussy as fast as he could.

Becca shouted out in delight as her pussy opened up and her juices started to flow readily on Dave's face. He greedily tried to drink every drop she squirted on to his face.

Jenn screamed out as her body exploded. Dave could feel her juices erupting on his throbbing cock and running over his cock and balls. Her rhythm slowing now as she slid easily up and down his rock hard cock.

Both of the women rolled off of Dave, impressed that he had not cum yet.

"Dave, I have to say you are just full of surprises! You can choose which pussy you want to cum inside first!" said Becca.

She was secretly hoping it would be her as even though she lost her cherry earlier, she had still never had cum inside of her body, and she craved it more than anything right now.

"Well, seeing as you are the birthday girl. I do believe it is only fitting that you be first!" He said with a large smile on his face.

Becca said nothing but leaned in and gave him a lustful deep kiss.

"Jenn, that means you are on the bed! Leg's wide open!" she said.

Jenn got on the bed and spread her legs wide as per instruction. Becca positioned her head between Jenn's legs and started to lick her pussy. Becca learned earlier that her ass needed to be pointed in the air and her head down low for sex from behind.

Dave came up behind Becca and placed his cock at her entrance. He pushed himself into her and slowly started to fuck her. She could feel mild discomfort from the stretching of Blake earlier in the day. But more than that should could feel the delight of Dave's cock deep inside of her body.

Becca kept on licking Jenn's clit as she slid two fingers inside of her slippery wet hole. Dave started to fuck Becca harder. Every thrust into her body forced Becca's face hard into Jenn's pussy. Jenn was quickly being brought to climactic heights again. She grabbed her own breasts and gave them a tight squeeze. She started moaning loudly and gasping for air. She wanted to hold back on her second orgasm but Becca was doing everything right.

Dave pounded Becca harder now. His cock slamming into her body deeply. Becca's pussy was dipping as she felt her juices running down the inside of her leg.

Jenn's body erupted. Her juices started to squirt on to Becca's face. Becca exploded as she could feel her juices gushing from her body.

Dave grabbed her hips hard and with one final thrust she felt his cock pulsing deep inside of her body. She felt the spray of his hot cum at the very depths of her pussy. She smiled as she enjoyed the sensation for the very first time in her life.

She gave Jenn one last lick to clean her juices from her pussy.

Dave pulled his cum stained cock from Becca and stood by the bed, unsure what to do next.

Becca stood up and helped Jenn off the bed.

Becca gave Dave a long French kiss. He could taste Jenn's juices on her lips and tongue. His hands began to play with her breasts as they made out for a few moments.

Becca dropped to her knees and took his cock into her mouth. She could taste their juices on his semi erect rod.

Jenn knelt beside her and reached over to fondle Becca's breast.

Becca released his cock only to have it picked up by Jenn. She took it into her mouth and skillfully massaged the underside of his rod with her tongue. She played with his cock in her mouth until he started to grow in her mouth.

She pushed him into the back of her throat and let the head of his dick enter her throat.

Becca looked on wishing she knew how to do that. Jenn released his cock and Becca took over. She started sucking his now fully erect cock and making sure each time she pushed him to the back of her throat. She tried to push his dick into her throat but her gag reflex kicked in and she had to release his cock.

"Becca, relax your throat. If you are tense you will choke! Here watch!" She said.

Jenn took his cock and slid it into her mouth. Once his head hit the back of her throat she relaxed and took his entire cock into her mouth right up to his balls pressed against her chin.

"Now you try!" she said.

Becca took his cock and allowed the head to reach her throat. She relaxed as best she could and slowly pushed his head into her throat. She was able to get some of his cock into her throat before she again started to choke.

"Relax! Don't think about it, or over think it. Just relax and let him in!" said Jenn.

Becca took him again. Again his head hit her throat. She relaxed and closed her eyes. His head pushed into her throat and a moment later his balls were pressed against her chin. Her eyes watering slightly from his head in her throat. She released his cock as she stroked it as she gasped for air.

"I did it! Dave how was that, did you like it?" she asked.

"Oh fuck yeah! You can practice deep throating my cock all night long if you like!" he replied.

Becca said nothing more but took his cock again and once more pushed it into her throat. She was quite proud of her newly learned skill and kept blowing him and allowing his dick into her throat over and over again.

"Oh fuck yeah!" Dave moaned as he was loving Becca's talents.

Jenn watched as Becca worked his cock hard. Her saliva dripping out the side of her mouth as she refused to stop sucking his dick. Dave ran his fingers through her hair as he moaned louder.

She felt the first blast of his cum in her throat. She opened her mouth and let his dick rest on her tongue like she did with Blake earlier in the day. Jenn watched as his cock twitched on her tongue and erupted lines of cum into her mouth. Jenn grabbed his dick and pointed it at her open mouth. His cock continued to shoot loads of cum into Jenn's mouth and chin. Dave took his dick in his hand and began stroking it. He aimed at both the women as his cock shot the last of his juices on to their tits.

Jenn grabbed Becca and kissed her hard. Both their mouths were filled with Dave's cum as they kissed and fought over his juices.

"So Dave! My parents will be gone until at least noon tomorrow! Care to spend the night with us?" asked Becca.

"Well, I would love to, but I have nothing to sleep in. If you don't mind me being naked all night!" he said with a playful smile.

"Oh that's fine! I wasn't planning on letting you get much sleep anyway!" she said.

The three of them burst out into laughter and hopped into her king sized bed.